For Moss

This is Mark.

Mark is an aardvark.

Mark is an aardvark
dressed as a shark.

This is Clark the meadowlark with
Mark the aardvark dressed as a shark.

Clark the meadowlark is wearing
a large scarf with Mark the aardvark
dressed as a shark.

Clark the meadowlark is wearing a large
scarf and makes art from a cart under
a tarp with Mark the aardvark
dressed as a shark.

There is a party in the park under the tarp, below the stars, and in the dark. It is about to start!

This is Darla with Mark the aardvark dressed as a shark and Clark the meadowlark wearing a large scarf, doing art from a cart under a tarp.

Darla is dressed as a candy bar and plays a guitar for the party in the park. It is time to start!

Darla came from the barn on the farm. The farm not far from the party at the park below the stars and in the dark.

Darla plays the guitar very hard while dressed as a large candy bar with Mark the aardvark dressed as a shark and Clark the meadowlark in his large scarf doing art from a cart.

Clark the meadowlark paints a dart in a heart. Darla says, "That is not art."

She thinks she is smart under that tarp with Clark the meadowlark wearing a large scarf and Mark the aardvark dressed as a shark for the party in the park, below the stars and in the dark.

They were just about to starve
when a martian arrived from Mars.
It saw the party on starship radar
and came from afar with a
jar of tar.

"It means no harm." said Mark, the
aardvark dressed as a shark, who
was charmed by the bizarre tar
from Mars on the party tarp.

In his large scarf, Clark stopped his
art to look at Darla, dressed as a
candy bar playing the guitar very
hard at the party in the park
under a tarp below the stars
and in the dark.

There they are with that jar of tar. The smell was harsh like a stink in a marsh.

"It smells like a fart." barked Mark the aardvark dressed as a shark, harkening to Clark the meadowlark, wearing a large scarf next to his art and cart.

Darla, from the barn on the farm, nearly barfed hard into her guitar, dressed as that candy bar at the party in the park under a tarp, below the stars, and in the dark.

Mark the aardvark thought it was smart to depart the party in the park under the stars and in the dark. The tar on the tarp's odor was sharp!

Although, Mark the aardvark dressed like a shark did very much like the dart in the heart made by Clark the meadowlark on the cart under the tarp.

Mark the aardvark thought it was art.

Made in the USA
Las Vegas, NV
03 May 2024

89469970R00019